HANDBOOK
TO A
HYPOTHETICAL
CITY

ALBERT RECHTS

HANDBOOK
TO A
HYPOTHETICAL
CITY

THE LILLIPUT PRESS

Copyright © Albert Rechts

All rights reserved. No part of this publication may be reproduced in any form or by any means without the prior permission of the publisher.

First published in 1986 by
THE LILLIPUT PRESS LTD
Gigginstown, Mullingar, Co. Westmeath, Ireland

British Library Cataloguing in Publication Data
Rechts, Albert
  Handbook to a hypothetical city.
  I Title
  828'.91408   PR6068.E2/
  ISBN 0 946640 15 7

Design by JARLATH HAYES
Cover illustration by HECTOR McDONNELL
Set in 11 on 12 Baskerville and printed by
BLACKROCK PRINTERS LTD, Blackrock, Co. Dublin

CONTENTS

- 7   Invocation
- 9   Preface
- 11   Introduction
- 12   Of fortifications
- 15   Of detritus
- 17   Of sects and sectaries
- 19   Some residents of the City: 1
- 21   Of winds, and weathers
- 22   Of private and public armies
- 26   Some residents of the City: 2
- 29   Of pipes and tubes
- 30   Of fire
- 33   Of sounds, and sights
- 35   Of the government of the City
- 38   Of work, or its lack: and of recreation
- 39   Some residents of the City: 3
- 42   Reflections on the preceding
- 43   Consequences of the preceding
- 47   Conclusions of this book

IN THE NAME OF ALLAH, THE COMPASSIONATE, THE MERCIFUL

I swear by this City (and you yourself (Mohammed) are a resident of this City), by the begetter (Adam) and all whom he begot: We created man to try him with afflictions.

. . . Have We not given him two eyes, a tongue, and two lips, and shown him the two paths? Yet he would not scale the Height.

Would that you knew what the Height is! It is the freeing of a bondsman; the feeding, in the day of famine, of an orphaned relation, or a needy man in distress; to have faith and to enjoin fortitude and mercy.

Those that do this shall stand on the right hand; but those that deny Our revelations shall stand on the left, with Hellfire close above them.

From the Koran, surah 90, 'The City': tr. N. K. Dawood.

PREFACE

This City, which has no reality, is therefore hard to pin down in place or time. As to place, let us say only that it seems to be somewhere in the northern hemisphere. As to time, this is even more difficult: not only because time itself is of its nature a fluid:* nor merely because the City often seems to exist in an alternative stream of history: but mostly because, in the time-dimension, the City seems constantly to be slipping and sliding backwards, and never quite able to make up what it has somehow lost.

Like any other city, it may be sliced and analysed in many different ways: horizontally, vertically, transversely, diagonally; but the fact is, that an imaginary city allows the invention of additional dimensions to suit every purpose. This book, therefore, represents a selection from the infinite number of possible alternative slices. Some of them are at a far remove from 'reality'; others may be so 'real' as to appear crude and brutal. Some lay claim, at one level or another, to being 'true': some are wholly hypothetical: some are deliberately falsified. Some belong to the peculiar world of — faction. Each, it is submitted, has a kind of validity of its own.

A.R.
July 1986

*Time, like an ever-rolling stream, bears all its sons away.

INTRODUCTION

Counting its suburbs, its outliers, and its dormitories, the City has a population of around half a million humans; about the same number of rats;* a rather smaller number of cats, dogs, parrots and budgies; a much larger number of bed-bugs, fleas, bluebottles and cockroaches. Every square centimetre of its surface is called upon to contribute its quota to the duty of supporting life, be its form higher or lower.

The City is bounded to the north by a mountain range of high fantastic pinnacles of hard black basalt. The paths and tracks up to the passes are steep, but not impenetrable. The tumbled plateau beyond the mountains affords a measure of shelter from the icy winds which, in winter, rush down from the polar north. However, in exchange, it attracts a shroud of murky cloud which too often strays southward and clings clammily to the northern quarters of the City.

To the east, the sea: grumbling, ebbing, flowing, sometimes overflowing, in the narrow channel of its fjord; deep; very tidal; clear and salty and savoury as oyster-juice when the wind is in the west, and the ordures of the City are scoured away far from land; brown, turgid, and laced with florescent algae and putrescent jelly-fishes when the east wind bottles up the excreta of the City in its narrow bay.

The sea's banks are, part, of ragged rocks; part, of man-made sea-walls propped against a shelf of blue clay; part, of rock-strewn mud; small part only, of beaches of shifting sand, evanescent as a powder made from finely ground hour-glasses. At the head of the estuary there are broad mud-flats, white-speckled with flying sheets of waste paper, and plastic cups, and scavenging gulls. Also, broad windswept acres of open rubbish tip, smelly and smoky, with a sub-population and sub-ecology all their own.

In the waters of the inlet, all-year round swimmers and their look-alikes, seals; porpoises, codfish, mackerel; terns, cormorants, oystercatchers, herons, and so on; bait-diggers; limpets, mussels, seaweeds, sea-bats, mermaids — and so forth.

---

*'One rat family to a household, and three fleas to a rat, seems to have been the norm' (Philip Ziegler, *The Black Death*).

Are these creatures to be counted amongst the population of the City? Yes; for the lives of sea and land are indivisible, interpenetrate: as witness the headstrongness of elvers in spring, trying to batter their way ashore, even through sea-walls, into the tingling inland amniotic headwaters.

To the south, rolling hills and downland, punctuated by the strong farms of stout loyal yeomen; then broad inland lakes; then a sky-high range of rounded granite mountains whose peaks are usually hidden from the City by cloud. Beyond those mountains, another country: to some of the people of the City, a Promised Land; to others, a foreign and menacing Unfriendly Power.

To the westward, the valley floor with its winding river leading to the mysterious and sinister interior: a thickly wooded corridor of level ground where the ghosts of gnarled and intermingled oak trees harbour the ghosts of wood-kerns and outlaws: where wild sows snuffle for acorns and pine-mast: where black clinging flies from the nearby lakes and marshes torment the already-nervous traveller in the spring and early summer.

And amidst all these, at the centre of the compass-rose, a saucerful of slob; a long-disused ford and a many-times-rebuilt bridge; stone-revetted quays and slipways, and the pool where the big ships turn; the disc of level mud, its water-table so high that the very basements burst out in sweat at the time of the spring tides; an elliptical rim of raised beaches; the curved and sloping braes leading up to the steeper mountain-sides; the arena, tier upon tier, contour upon contour, looking down upon the open stage which is the heart and centre of the City.

OF FORTIFICATIONS

The City is encrusted with fortifications of every date; past, present, and (very likely) future. Contrary to normal archaeological usage, the most ancient stratum is at the very top: the bones of a waterless stone-and-turf promontory fort perched on the highest crag of the peak overlooking the ford. Some way down the near-sheer cliff face, a series of natural caves, slightly enhanced by prehistoric artifice, exhibit traces of bone and stonecraft; but these are not strictly martial works. A few hundred yards farther down the same escarpment is a two-hundred-year old bivouac known as the Musketeers' Well.

Lower down, on the hills surrounding the inner plain, there are the remains of eight-hundred year old motte-and-bailey forts, only one of them in good preservation, and that colonised by a tall clump of trees. Here small boys and their dogs scramble up, and slide intemperately down, the steep slopes of the tall earth-mound, its wooden palisadoes long since crumbled to dust. On a smaller scale, hillocks and drumlins throughout the built-up area are, or were, surmounted by the raths indigenous to this country, rings of turf wall and ditch enclosing defensible farmsteadings. More enigmatic is the great brooding elliptical earthwork overlooking the river valley, the Druids' Ring, enclosing a space of several acres, with a megalith at its centre.

At the heart of the old town there stood, four hundred years ago, commanding first the ford and then the long many-arched stone bridge, a squat stone church with a square fortified tower; and a tall stone castle, with pistol-loups, mullions and high chimneys, set in a complex of yards, orchards and gooseberry-gardens, surrounded by stout walls. Of these no visible trace remains, though the name lives on: the elaborate new castle, built a century past in the deerpark on the lower slopes of the mountain, was not designed for defence, though in times of open warfare it was commandeered by seafaring men since, from its high terraces, ships approaching, entering or leaving the mouth of the fjord could be entrapped in the long brass cylinders of their telescopes.

In the Troubled Times of three to four centuries ago, the then town was fortified: girt about with stone-faced walls, twenty feet high, with inner wall-walks, guarded gates, and polygonal bastions. Although these walls were, by degrees, dismantled over the years at the instance of over-optimistic men of commerce, they have in more modern Troubled Times reappeared in slightly different guise, but along almost precisely the old lines. Now they take the form of tall steel arrow-tipped railings, topped by coils of barbed wire, interrupted at intervals by heavily padlocked gates for ingress; and clattering seven-foot turnstiles for egress; so that the innermost circle of the city can be garrisoned, isolated, and protected from intruders.

There are, scattered throughout the City, other defensive structures of various kinds and degrees of permanence. At some periods, the citizenry in their embattled enclaves have built barricades of paving-stones and cars, lorries and omnibuses, often burned or burning, around the sacred boundaries of the indicated territory. Such obstacles have mostly been transitory. More permanent, more linear, are the Eirenic Walls staking out the boundaries between tribal homelands. Sometimes, these are high corrugated-iron fences. In such cases, they may (on both sides) provide the groundwork for the embellishments of graffitists. Elsewhere, they have become genuine walls, usually of brick, often as much as fifteen feet high, usually treated with some form of surface graffito-deterrent; intended accordingly to shield and protect those who must live, so to speak, in the shadow of the wall, from the greater exuberance and pugnacity of those who live on what must be (by definition) its upper side.

Many individual buildings are, to a greater or a lesser degree, fortified. The bureaux of the gendarmerie are provided with high screens of steel-mesh netting, sand-bags, and gate-houses with splayed loop-holes. Likewise, the barracks of cavalry, infantry and marines, and their outposts: equipped with high screens, still higher signal-masts, and roof-top sangars; at their gates, chicanes of concrete slabs or cement-filled tubs, humps in the roadway, yellow floodlights. Outside the barracks used by the militia, and some of the main administrative quarters of the City, stand strong-points fetchingly disguised as ornamental gate-lodges. The houses of persons of importance — the Strato-pedarch, the Lords Justice, the Protospatharius — have toughened glass, stout doors, bright lights, guards dozing by the kitchen stove, fierce dogs. The houses occupied by the underground leaders of subversion, the commanders-in-chief of the private armies and their jingling chiefs of staff, are similarly sensitised, if less conspicuous. The meeting-places of the warring guilds, rightly or wrongly believed to be the warehouses for instruments of unauthorised violence, are at all times guarded by tilers within and without.

Private citizens who feel themselves to be, in the least degree, vulnerable to blackmail, theft, kidnapping, extortion, torture, or just plain old-fashioned assassination, take their own precautions. This is a city of fear; a city of blinds drawn down, and curtains drawn across; of shuttered windows; of stoutly framed doors with fish-eye spy-holes; of television scanners askew above the porch; mirrors showing, through the fanlight, the bald pate of the visitor on the door-mat; and entry-phones in place of bells and knockers.

OF DETRITUS

Detritus, like dirt, being a kind of matter misplaced, takes many forms. Where does dust come from? Yet dust is, save in a vacuum, universal and inescapable. The City is not exempt from the steady, relentless, eternal, silent yet choking fall of dust, which has over slow millennia completely buried not just other cities, but whole civilisations. Still, this City more than most redistributes its dustfalls at intervals — no way of doing this more effective than the judicious use of explosives.

One of the constituent elements of dust is soot; another, ash. 'Ashes to ashes, dust to dust.' The combustions of the city contribute their share to its overburden. Not just the bonfires of which this handbook writes elsewhere; not just the output of domestic and industrial chimneys; but also the slow fires of rubbish-tip, burning-ghat, and crematorium. Though the corpse of the beloved, in its brass-bound coffin, may be lowered discreetly from the crematory chapel to the boiler-room below; though the canned music may mask the roar of the gas-jets; yet after the shaking of hands and the deciphering of labels on wreaths, the debouchment into the frosty air is accompanied by puffs of dark smoke from the half-hidden chimney; which descend as minute particles of the beloved upon the head and clothing of the bereaved; who all unknowing carries them henceforth with him — 'dust to dust', indeed! Or, if he be too urgent in his desire to escape from the place of burning, then these same particles will gradually fertilise the gardens and fields around.

Or: there are alternative funerary customs. There is burial in long barrows, or round barrows, or chambered cairns, or horned cairns. There is hydrotaphia, or urn-burial. There is sepulture in one of the great sprawling cemeteries of the City — wide acres of toppling tombstones, their encomiastic downfall hastened by impious vandalism. Tramps, drunks and addicts use these aedicules, or cottages of the grave, as handy places for sleeping, drinking, and sniffing this drug or that glue; motocyclists use the humps and hollows of grave-surround and cavity as a race-track; lovers take refuge between the yews, the hollies, and the obelisks (Man is born to die: how many infants, legitimate or illegitimate, have been conceived in the graveyards of the City?); florists' flowers and wreaths unexpectedly seed themselves and prosper in this fertile ground; the grave-diggers' bee-hives and bean-rows flourish in ridge-and-furrow silhouette; there are special grave-plots for phalangists, and ayatollahs, and political prisoners, and those who have died of anti-social diseases such as cholera, typhoid, yellow fever, blackjack, and AIDS – though not for syphilis, gonorrhea, cancer, or melancholy-mania, regarded as quite conventional and acceptable modes of death.

Not only are there mortuary chapels; and places in houses of worship for the lying-in-state of cadavers; and funeral parlours (astounding expression: Will you come into my parlour? said the spider to the fly); there is also the municipal morgue; and there are the refrigerated cupboards of the forensic surgeons who assist the coroner in the coronation of death by violence.

And these are the death-places only of humans; consider also the municipal abattoir, where vegetarians recoil from the daily abattrement of pigs, sows, stirks, cows, calves, sheep, and woolly little lambs. Not to mention the veterinary establishments where pollicle dogs and jellicle cats are 'put to sleep'; and the, occasional, animals' graveyards where their corpses, along with those of beloved chargers or hunters or ponies, may be laid to rest: in contrast to the fate of foxes, rats, mice, badgers, hedgehogs, ferrets, weasels, hares, rabbits, frogs, toads, and other ferae naturae, which must await the resurrection of the body (if such there be, for them or any sentient creature) from the indignity of the rubbish dump.

The City is surrounded by its tips. Some are in worked-out quarries in the ring of surrounding hills, or in the valleys carved by the streams that run down from them; filthy messes of ash, metal, plastic, wood, paper, and deliquescent animal and vegetable matter. The largest are sited beside the sewage farms and outfalls on the seashore where, at the head of the fjord, endless acres are yearly reclaimed from the tide by the dumping of detritus of every kind. Here the seagulls, no longer fish-eaters, swoop and scream in thousands; here they ingest strange new botulisms; here the occasional unsuspected human corpse festers and rots amidst animal remains, abandoned perambulators, bottomless buckets and burned-out motor-cars, tins, bottles, packages, used contraceptives; old tax returns, love-letters, undergarments, odd shoes; hopes, ambitions, aspirations, fears, tears, and despairs.

Some of these, at least, are supposed to have been burned in the City's municipal incinerator: which indeed puffs away dark smoke like a second but non-human crematorium. Much which should go there fails to do so. But in the end, dust and soot apart, most of the physical substance both of City and of living citizens (including hair-cuttings, nail-clippings, and excreta) ends up either in the incinerator; or in the enormous sewage works nearby; or on the seaside tip. And, amongst the three, the final (short of resurrection) end-product is an unsavoury smell; a foul reek of decay, chemical reaction and putrescence: which enrages those citizens who live nearby. The Eparchs have installed numerous, but unsuccessful, expedients: mass-produced deodorants: lye: acids: fumigators: incense burners and joss-sticks: nets: screens: quicklime: and even electronic smell deflectors: but without success. It must be admitted that, in certain airs and in certain directions, the City is no more sweet-smelling physically than it is morally.

But that in no way discourages the longshoremen who sally forth at low tide onto the mudbanks just below the tips and outfalls: who, with plastic buckets and curving farm-forks, dig by daylight, by dusk, or by acetylene lamps after dark or before dawn, for the fat and juicy lugworms which flourish and grow large on the distillations of the detritus of the City.

OF SECTS AND SECTARIES

The people of the City are for the most part of one race (though some of them would deny it); yet amongst them are a great multitude of sects, creeds, and societies. Seafaring men of all nations pass through the fjord and the port; and here, as elsewhere, there are communities of dark or yellow-skinned immigrants from other continents. They have brought with them lodges of the great international secret societies — the mafia, the camorra, the triads, the yakuza, the freemasons, the Knights of Malta, the order of St John of Jerusalem. Alongside these, competing local and indigenous organisations flourish amazingly. Like the chariot-racing factions of Constantinople, they are distinguished by the colours they flaunt: green, yellow, purple, orange, black, scarlet. In different quarters of the City, the colours commanding local loyalty are often daubed on the walls, the roadways, the individual kerb-stones. Some, and these do not flaunt their colours, are genuinely secret societies; others say they are open societies with secrets; others again assert that they are hermetic religious organisations.

It is no easy matter to distinguish the religious from the secular. Almost every street in the City has its temples, its mosques, churches, mesjids, chapels, tabernacles, halls, lodges, and more secretive meeting-places. Some are of marble, of granite, of exquisite tilework; others are crude and humble shacks. Some have soaring minarets, gilded domes, spires, cupolas, campaniles, pinnacled towers; pediments, columns, pilasters, pendentives, squinches. In some, the tessellated pavements are covered in layer upon layer of rich overlapping carpets, the gifts of the faithful; the mihrabs glow with the colours of Iznik; venerable grandfather clocks stand against the walls, pendulums appearing and disappearing tick by tock in their shadowy lenticles; racks of vacant shoes outside the door.

The greater number of the inhabitants of the City embrace the Sunnī doctrine; but the Shī'as constitute a very sizeable minority. Apart from the other creeds – there are Jews, Copts, Christians, Nestorians, Buddhists, Maronites, Baha'i, Sikhs, Hindus, Confucians, Theosophists, and British Israelites – there are innumerable sub-denominations or sects of the principal creeds. Of course, all Shī'as believe their Imam to possess superhuman qualities derived from Adam the forefather through Muhammad; that his body throws no shadow; and that it cannot be physically harmed; but there remains room for a myriad differences. A'isha reports that the prophet never urinated when standing; whereas Hudhayfa reports that he did so. It is accordingly not surprising that amongst the denominations in the City are to be numbered Zaydis, Qādiānīs, and Mu'tazilites, covering a great spectrum between broad and narrow church; Twelvers who impatiently await the second coming of Muhammad al-Mahdi; Druzes, believed (despite or because of their penchant for massacring Christians) to have tenets in common with the freemasons; a few survivors of the hashish-eating Assassins, followers of the Old Man of the Mountains; members of that other very secret society, the Ismā'ilīya; and those Old Believers, the Ahmadıya, who consider all innovation in matters religious culpable, and who contribute to the maintenance of the burial-place of Jesus Christ in Srinagar.

Of course, this wide diversity in practice and belief greatly favours a high level of employment amongst the clerical and ecclesiastical classes. Every creed must have its Caliph and Cadi; every sect must have imam, mullah, mufti or fatwah; ayatollahs abound; faquirs and dervishes, being in good demand, are naturally in good supply; presumably the same holds good for jinns, those creatures of fire, intermediate between men and angels, who may be either bad or good.

The preoccupation with religion in the City is, thus, very great; people devote to it the attention which, in other places, they might squander upon horse-races or football pools. Whether this state of affairs is good or bad, is a matter of debate: but that it has consequences for the way of life of the City and its citizens, cannot be doubted.

SOME RESIDENTS OF THE CITY: 1

The Hajji Ishaq is a green-turbanned Sunnī who has made his pilgrimage to Mecca, and so can afford a grain of tolerance: of course, not overmuch. He does not love his Shī'a confreres, but at least makes a half-hearted effort to do so. For, having moved in the more generous airs of the wider world, he is prepared to believe that some of them may be misguided rather than deliberately wicked; deluded rather than sinful; misled rather than mis-leaders.

Yet, he has his doubts.

* * * * *

The Ayatollah Omar is a cleric of a very different kidney: a most vociferous demagogue with a rousing and, sometimes, indelicate turn of phrase; who both feeds, and feeds upon, the excesses of his following of zealots. He has only to use the words 'unclean', 'Kafir', 'infidel', 'Giaour', to have his congregation straining at the leash; and then let every male hearer look to the appropriate furnishing (or unfurnishing) of his prepuce.

Omar is a Sunnī fundamentalist: not a man for sophistries, nor for counting the number of jinns who may dance on the point of a pin. He is a purveyor of faith rather than works. He learned his trade in the tents of the desert – not unlike circus tents, not unlike gospel tents – where healing and other miraculous sacraments are not unknown.

In private life, amidst the hospitable bosoms of his lawful wives, Omar is not an unamiable, is indeed an uxorious man. But once he rises to preach, he is a very different and a very formidable person.

* * * * *

The Holy Suleiman is a Shī'a first and foremost, a fully paid-up member of the Party of God. Those who share his own beliefs are entitled to his utmost loyalty; no good word of a Sunnī may be spoken with safety in his hearing. If there is one thing which engorges his great jowls with rage, it is a mixed marriage between members of the two communities.

For to his mind, every Sunnī is not just misguided, but utterly and irretrievably damned to eternal perdition. From which in turn it follows that all their words and deeds are odious, culpable, and beyond all human forgiveness: though just conceivably, Allah, the Compassionate, the Merciful, may forgive where right-thinking humans dare not do so.

* * * * *

Silken Thomas is a cleric of smooth tongue: as it sometimes seems, all things to all men. There are those who love him as a genial and devoted peacemaker, bringing together members of the warring sects. There are those who loathe him as traitor for doing so. There are others again who simply despise him as a canting hypocrite.

Silken Thomas hunts both with the hare and the hounds. Needless to say, the one never gets caught by the other when he is around: which is always something to be thankful for.

* * * * *

Brother Janus is a most saintly man. If he is two-faced, then it must be acknowledged that both his faces are devout. In the pulpit he is a scourge of vice, especially sexual vice, in all its forms. In the confessional, provided the truth, the whole truth, and nothing but the truth are laid out before him in full, he is more charitable and forgiving; and very adept in the adumbration of really appropriate penances.

* * * * *

The Archimandrite Chrysanthemos is above all these things. Bless him, he lives in a dream world all of his own, somewhere half-way between the island of Patmos and the Book of Revelations. The souls of the City entrusted to his care revere and adore him, since he is so very holy and unworldly. But they do not find it helpful to seek, still less to follow, his advice in matters temporal. And who shall blame them?

*   *   *   *   *

Brother Irenæus and Brother Pax Vobiscum are two very passionate and zealous Shī'ites. Not for them the diplomacies, the wiles, the courtesies, of their ecclesiastical superiors. They write joint or several letters to the press at least once a week, castigating the present and (especially) the past misfeasances of the enemy majority, and of the forces charged with keeping the peace between the two sides. They have little talent for distinguishing motes from beams; but they derive vast job-satisfaction from their self-imposed task.

As to their own fairness and impartiality, one could no more deprive them of these estimable qualities than one could steal a keyhole.

OF WINDS, AND WEATHERS

The City, physically if not spiritually, enjoys a temperate climate. It is scoured by healthy and cleansing winds, its buenos aires. It is spared the extremes of heat and drought, of blizzard and permafrost; which is not to say that hot sunshine and heavy snowfalls are unknown; nor that the weather plays no part in the life of the City.

The prevailing winds are west or south-westerly; fresh, humid, travellers from the Gulf Stream as single-minded as eels from the weedy Sargasso; bowling along before them clouds of every size and shape, high and low, thick and thin, white and black and of a million shades of luminous grey. For this is not a tropical region of constant blue skies; on the contrary, the amphitheatre of the City is roofed and ceilinged by an ever-changing kaleidoscopic canvas of over-sailing clouds against a farthest blue. Or, at dusk and dawn, the more vivid colours of shepherd's delight or shepherd's warning. Or, at night, the hemisphere as of a planetarium.

The westerly winds bring, not just clouds, but rain: ranging from downpours and flash-floods, two or three times each twelvemonth, to the soft moist mist, too fine and imperceptible to be called a drizzle, characteristic of much of the year. The people of the City are well acclimatised to rain; it soothes and mollifies, to some extent, their quarrelsome passions; its absence for a longer-than-usual dry spell sets their nerves on edge, and gives rise to almost sexual tensions.

Easterly winds are of two kinds: in summer, hot, dry, dusty, and odorous, marking a settled spell of fine weather; in winter, sharp, bitter, freezing gales all the way from the Chorasmian wastes, that clutch and tear at chimney-pots, roof-slates, sea-walls, and any structures whose repair and good order have been neglected.

Northerly and southerly winds, in accordance with the laws of nature in their application to the hemispheres, are warm and caressing, or chilly and abrasive, as the case may be.

Fogs there are; and mists; also hard frosts, and ice; driving sleet and pounding hail; but within historic memory, no tidal waves, earthquakes or tsunamis; nor is there any active volcano near the City: which, in truth, has no need of one.

OF PRIVATE AND PUBLIC ARMIES

If the people of the City are for the most part of one race – descendants of one or another generation of far-flung adventurers from the steppes – it is quite otherwise in the matter of nationhood. Different clans are proud to claim descent from the Avars, the Huns, the Goths, the Vandals. But over-ridingly, the citizens are divided into two broad factions. The larger of these claims descent from, and asserts its undying allegiance to, Tamburlaine the Mongol, and his Golden Horde.* But the more purist faction dismisses the Mongols as Johnny-come-latelys, and

---

*'Timur (or Tamerlane) the Mongol, an old white-haired cripple from the far east, an intellectual specialist in chess, theology, and conquest, and perhaps the greatest artist in destruction known in the savage annals of mankind.' (1355-1405; H. A. L. Fisher, 'History of Europe'.)

asserts with equal passion its descent from, and its eternal loyalty to, Genghiz Khan and the Tartar princes of a far earlier generation.§

To complicate matters, the Tartars claim links of kinship and nationhood with the race living just beyond the range of granite mountains to the south of the City; while the Mongols claim similar links with the peoples settled in the Eastern Isles of the adjacent archipelago.

To complicate matters further, most, but not all, of the Tartars are Shī'as; whereas most, but not all, of the Mongols are Sunnīs.

And to complicate matters further still, each party is totally and immovably convinced of its own unique rightness: and therefore feels itself beyond all question morally justified in bearing, and indeed employing, arms against those fellow-citizens who hold other views.

The governors of the City are therefore constrained (some most unwillingly, some with almost excessive zeal) to keep on foot a standing army, with legions of auxiliaries; the 'forces of law and order', comprising not only soldiers, seamen and airmen, but also frogmen, dogmen and firemen; gendarmes, carabinieri, carbonari, hetmans, hussars, and land and water bailiffs. And so, those who lack power feel themselves authorised to raise private armies for, as they see it, their protection and that of their innocent unarmed womenfolk, children and clergy, against vile and tyrannical oppression.

There is accordingly within the City at any given moment a state of potential, if not actual, civil war: comparable to the mode of existence of a volcano which is neither extinct, nor permanently active: sometimes quiescent, sometimes snoring gently, sometimes emitting mere wisps of smoke, then puffs, then clouds; sometimes mere driblets of lava, then streamlets, then roaring burning rivers; sometimes light powders of ash, then plumes, then falls of red-hot snow such as choked and overwhelmed the populace of Pompeii.

§'The Tartars were no undisciplined horde of feckless barbarians, but a force of some half a million trained light horsemen, representing an empire which in the lifetime of Jingis Khan, its creator, had been extended from Manchuria to the Caucasus at a cost of more than eighteen million lives. No empire had ever occupied so large a portion of the earth's surface as that of Jingis, or had been the cause of so much human suffering in the winning.' (1162-1227; H. A. L. Fisher.)

Such, indeed, may in the end be the fate of the City. In the meanwhile, armies and guerillas come and go, mostly by night. In some, the officers are idealistic and high-minded patriots, while the rank and file are made up of a surly mixture of criminals and louts. In others, the reverse is the case: officers and leaders are cynical self-seeking manipulators; rank and file are simple, honourable, high-minded warriors for 'freedom' as they understand it. Others again, and not the least dangerous, are shifting alliances of persons mentally diseased – the paranoid, the psychotic, the schizophrenic, the power-crazed. Others still are gangs of starry-eyed fanatics, blazing with the monomania of righteousness. And a few, a very occasional few (although the authorities dare never to admit it), may consist of rational and balanced ameliorationists, earnestly persuading themselves that their ends justify their means; and so pursuing, with intelligence and courage, objectives which they could never hope, alas, to obtain by peaceful and legitimate means: nor to hold, if once obtained by murderous and illegitimate ones.

Means and ends: ends and means. The modes of debate, in more civilised places and at more civilised times, do not include weapons. But this City is not such a place; nor is this such a time. Weapons may be of many kinds. Some are designed as such: rifles, pistols, machine-guns, sub-machine guns, sub-sub-machine guns, rocket launchers; bullets of lead or platinum or rubber or plastic, rockets, tear-gas canisters, hand grenades. These, for the private armies, are laborious to acquire, purchase or steal, and to smuggle into the City. But they confer the coveted cachet of professional status; like aircraft, helicopters, tanks, armoured cars, artillery and warships, they are only obtainable by those who are already rich and powerful.

But then, there are other kinds of weapon. For example: milk bottles or, better still, the largest size of glass sweetie-jars, half-filled with petrol, fused with a twisted rag, set alight, and dropped on passing cop-cars. Or: home-made catapults or cross-bows, firing bolts or ball-bearings with much precision over long distances. Or: small, easily hidden firebombs, made from tape cassettes, phosphorus, spring clothes pegs, or condoms filled with acid. Or: the big explosive bombs made from weed-killer stuffed into milk-churns, or oxygen cylinders, or steel beer-kegs; with nails or screws or bolts bought by the pound from the local ironmonger; and fuse or cortex, and cheap wrist-watch or alarm clock, electrical command wire or radio beam.

All, capable of striking man, woman or child very dead indeed; just as dead, indeed, as lies within the capability of nuclear explosion, or cholera, or hypothermia, or an agonising cancer of the bowel, or just old age: for dead is dead is dead: and we shall all, without doubt, be dead, sooner or later.

But: sooner: or later? That is the question. Because in most other places, people prefer later; but here in the City, a good many people express a preference for sooner; at least, insofar as concerns those whom they do not like.

* * * * *

Both public and private armies require logistical support: which at least has the virtue of generating widespread employment in the City. Even the smallest unit has need of recruiting and training staff (usually grizzled veterans) if only to ensure the replacement of casualties. There is always a need for volunteers with some medical or first-aid training; and, at times, for malleable doctors who can be blackmailed or cajoled into undertaking, so to speak, clandestine operations. There must be paymasters, commissariat and quartermasters, even if uniform consists of no more than beret, black gloves, and stocking mask; or combat-jacket, armband, desert cap and dark glasses: as the case may be.

A transport unit may be wanted, even though the hijacking of cars or motor-bicycles as required is so easy that it can usually be left to the teenage cubs or brownies. There may be a requirement for a service company or 'sweeney' to provide miscellaneous supporting and disciplinary functions. There will certainly be need of an armourer, and no doubt a skilled explosives artificer. And, undoubtedly, there must be an intelligence officer, with his network of agents, moles, sleepers, and retained informants. To add to the rich confusion, there will be the spies and agents of rival networks, and of foreign powers, seeking to penetrate and interpenetrate and plant double and treble agents; and pressmen, and photographers, and vicarious missionaries, and stray politicians, and young international revolutionaries: all or any of whom may also be in the businesses of buying or selling, imparting, disseminating, or collecting, information (or of course mis- or dis-information).

An army, public or private, is an expensive commodity, as robber barons, monarchs and dictators have discovered for themselves in other places and other times. An 'official' army can be provided with the sinews of war by tax collector, excise gauger, douanier and vatman. For the high command of a private army, rather more enterprise and business acumen may be required. Fund-raising charities may not provide the whole answer, though appeals for war widows and orphans, the wounded, prisoners' dependants, and refugees, can be tear-jerking and remunerative, especially if the proceeds can be diverted in their entirety to more military purposes. The management of sports or drinking clubs; the provision of taxi or dolmus services; the manipulation of dog-tracks and race-courses; the raising of funds by racketeering, or drug-pushing, or blackmail, or kidnapping, or extortion; if all else fails to provide the needful sums, plain unvarnished armed robbery whenever and wherever the opportunity presents itself: these are the incidents and accidents inseparable from the military traditions of the City.

SOME RESIDENTS OF THE CITY: 2

Pius and Innocenta are in the back bedroom of the flat this afternoon, making long and voluptuous love. Both are young, both are unemployed, the days are very long. Since each has an enviable innate talent for sex, they practise as often and for as long as they can, despite the fact that they do not at all care for each other: she dislikes his arrogance: he dislikes her sluttishness. Nevertheless, at this moment, she is straddling him, her knees gripping his thin flanks while she raises and lowers herself, lingeringly. Naturally, she is on the pill.

In the evenings, they both work for a locally based charitable organisation at a modest honorarium. Pius is employed to break the legs of drug-pushers, child molesters, and those who choose the wrong cars to steal; for this purpose, he is provided with a curved wooden bat. Innocenta is a courier, carrying sports-equipment bags containing weapons from the premises of wholesaler-in-violence to those of retailer; and vice versa.

Many right-thinking people of the same persuasion would, if they knew of them, regard the day-time activities of Pius and

Innocenta as much more reprehensible, and much less easily to be condoned, than their activities after nightfall.

* * * * *

Uel and Drew, Wesley and Winston, are in the back room of the so-called social club, spinning out their pints of lager with prudent thrift. All are in their mid-twenties; all are lucky enough to have jobs, though not very well-paid ones – shop assistant, caretaker, petrol pump attendant, security man. They are all honest and industrious; good husbands and fathers; bone-headed and loveable; if they have a fault at all, it is that each of them is a murderer many times over.

Their occasional twinges of conscience are not, however, so severe as the occasional twinges of beer-induced heart-burn. After all, they believe it to be their incontrovertible duty to their own community to rid it of its fanatical enemies.

Many right-thinking people of the same persuasion would, if they knew of them, regard their activities after dark as far more laudable than the humdrum daily virtues they display in the work-place and the home.

* * * * *

Doc Pat is a devoted jogger. In his nice clean track-suit, with the papers evidencing his professional standing tucked into the inside pocket, he trots daily around the suburban streets: who could have any suspicions of a physician so innocently engaged? Yet, being endowed with a photographic memory, he contrives each day to inspect the homes of judges, prosecutors, officers of gendarmerie and militia, bureaucrats and public officials: to note the times and routes of their comings and goings: the registration numbers of their cars: and such other particulars as an intending assassin might wish to know. What is more, in the course of his daily jog, he is able, always without suspicion, to call and deliver messages at such safe houses, armouries, and intelligence centres as may lie along his route.

In between times, Doc Pat devotes himself, in accordance with his Hippocratic oath, to the succouring of the sick, the comforting of the dying. For him, jogging, and the incidental activities that go with it, are no more than a hobby.

* * * * *

Captain Buck Black (generally known, with indrawn breath, as 'the Buck') is the commanding officer of the City Defence Force, the predominant pro-Mongol paramilitary formation. He is a very small but bristly man, rather untidy, at least one side of his spectacles usually fastened by a shoe-lace looped over a rather prominent ear; with a slow, precise, heavily accented voice; and exceptionally steely eyes. He is little known to the public, or even to his own followers, since he prefers to employ middle-men, front-men and spokesmen both for his pronunciamentos and for his military orders.

Nevertheless, he is a figure of terror. The unemotional theorist and intellectual of his faction, he has dealt with absolute ruthlessness with rivals or contradictors within his own ranks: if he is icy in dealing with his own people, he is sub-arctic in dealing with his enemies.

The Buck is a lonely figure. He has no woman, no confidante, no catamite, no friend. He lives, under the constant protection of trusty but uncomprehending guards, in an austere flat in a half-deserted housing estate in the rat-infested heartland of Mongol territory. It is said, but has never been proved, that he keeps a small pack of rats as pets; finding in their fine qualities of intelligence, self-sufficiency and unemotional stoicism, inspiration for his own courses of conduct.

* * * * *

Billy, William and Liam are all highly skilled artificers, scientifically trained in the use of firearms, ammunition and explosives. Their talents are much in demand. The skills of Liam and Billy are at the service of the opposing paramilitary factions to which they respectively adhere. They both received their training in the same schools as William, Liam having perjured himself and joined the ranks of his enemies for that express purpose.

William is a Technical Officer in the ordnance branch of the state security forces. Liam holds the rank of Company Armourer amongst the Tartar volunteers. Billy is a Sergeant-Technician with the corresponding Mongol organisation. They are not acquainted with each other; but they know each others' handiwork, and have a sincere respect for it. In general, it is Liam and Billy who devise and construct the implements of murder, ingenious and perilous to all who handle them – their manufacturers included. It is generally William whose terrifying task it is to defuse and neutralise them. It is hard to say which of the three has the longest expectation of life: there is a kind of running tontine between the three of them, but with bare survival as the only prize.

OF PIPES AND TUBES

What you see in this, or any, City depends upon how you choose to slice it. If you were to give our rumbling, grumbling, sickly City a barium meal and then X-ray it, you might be surprised. Medical text-books contain gaudy diagrams demonstrating the human structure in terms of arteries, veins, wind-pipes and intestines. The City, too, depends for its very life on an invisible network of pipes, tubes, cables and conduits; it is possible that the human race owes even more to the inventor of the pipe than to the inventor of the wheel.

Close your eyes, and imagine that everything else in the City has been blotted out: all that remains is a cats' cradle of thick or thin white lines which snake and coil their tangled courses around this enormous X-ray. The most prominent are the underground streams and rivers, sometimes flowing in culverts, sometimes in deep dirty ditches concealed from easy view; and the innumerable rivulets, streamlets, shores and field drains running down from the surrounding hills.

And then, the storm-water drains, overflows, and main sewers, some of them requiring the help of pumping stations at times of spring tide, or when thunderstorms have caused flash-flooding. And then, the lesser sewers, street by street, back alley by back garden; connecting with the individual house sewers; connecting in turn with individual U-bends, pissoirs, pans, bidets, and bowls; and so, ultimately, with the internal tubing of the citizens themselves.

And the gutters and downspouts. And the water mains and aqueducts – bringing in supplies this time, not carrying them away – from the lakes and reservoirs of the surrounding countryside, to thousands upon thousands of standpipes and taps in bathrooms, bedrooms, or kitchens. And hot water pipes, and cisterns, and hot cylinders, and boilers, and radiators. And gas mains, and pipes, and distributors; and district heating mains, and pipes, and distributors; and electricity main cables, and local cables, and wires, and conduits tracked into walls, and under floors, and behind skirting-boards; and telephone cables and wires and handsets: and all the items of electrical equipment at the ends of the wires, each with its own internal complexities, even if not all so many as in computers and micro-chips and word processors.

Imagine the most complex of miniaturised electronic circuit-boards; enlarge it to the size of the entire City; eliminate all irrelevancies; what is left is a weird construction of pipes and tubes and cables that coils its way intricately in, under, over and through the humps and hollows of the City. There is an austere kind of romance even to municipal plumbing: how much more so when the contents of all these channels are brought into account. Drinking water inwards and upwards; rain water downwards and outwards. Human wastes of every kind outwards, sizzling electrical currents inwards. Hot water steaming, and circulating, and cooling as it goes. The constant inward and outward traffic of telephone conversations about love, lust, sickness, business, gossip, death, all the exigencies of human existence.

Not to mention piped muzak; or organ-pipes; or tobacco-pipes; or bagpipes; in none of which is the City lacking.

OF FIRE

Fire, as an element, holds an exceptional fascination for the people of this City; and not just as a source of warmth in cold weather. Though indeed, there is a hearth in almost every home; indirect modes of heating are disliked and despised. In the poorest houses, the hearth is required to burn symbolically all year round, even in stifling summery weather when others put on their lightest clothing, and find any external source of heat oppressive. The eternal flames of the traditional hearth-stones are somehow kept alight by day and night, by the use of coal, coke, or anthracite, when they can be paid for; scantlings and brushwood, turfs and dried camel-dung, chair-legs and banister-rails, when times are hard.

The cooking-flame burns constantly under the kettle or

samovar of hospitality.

Great fires are built, too, as a mode of communal celebration. At certain seasons, and at the time of certain feasts, these fires assume astonishing proportions. Are they in some degree reminiscences of the ancient fires of Beltane and St John's Eve? When aromatic plants (thyme, camomile, fennel, geranium, penny-royal) were burned on the threshing-floors, and their smoke enriched and fertilised both ploughland and pasture; when barren cattle were driven back and forth through the embers; when young couples leaped thrice over the flames to ensure fertility; when effigies, lundies, wicker giants, were immolated in the leaping flames? Or survivals of the Need-fires lit in times of plague, pestilence, or calamity, which must be kindled (all other flames within the townland being first extinguished) by boy and girl, aged between eleven and fourteen, working stark naked to rub sticks together in a totally darkened room? However that may be, on a stated name-day, throughout the Mongol quarters of the City, enormous bonfires blaze all night at every street corner. Their construction takes many weeks: they may tower twenty or thirty feet tall, built by children and adolescents of the quarter out of old chests and boxes, beams and rafters, motor tyres, broken furniture and strayed sofas, paper, and the branches or even trunks of growing trees.

This season is the despair of those who cherish the City's gardens, private or municipal; marauding bands of looters and vandals invade and despoil orchards, garths, groves, hedgerows and parks; indeed, by far the greatest part of the fuel for these pyres consists of stolen goods. It is often found necessary to set guards over these piles, lest the builders of rival fires come by stealth in the dark to rob them; also, lest enemies of some other faction creep up to set them prematurely on fire before the proper feast-day. Small boys, fallen asleep on sentry-duty, are in many years thus roasted alive in their nests.

On the night itself, as summer darkness falls slowly, one by one the bonfires are set alight: until all the Mongol districts of the City are atwinkle with flames and surmounted by columns of dark smoke: while the citizenry, and especially the younger people, dance, drink, sing, fornicate, carouse and rejoice around the fires. As the flames leap higher, as the gouts of black oily smoke become more and more interspersed with sparks and sherds of incandescent paper, so the nearest homes are at ever-increasing risk; their occupants desperately dash buckets of water over smoking walls and singed woodwork; but sometimes in vain, so voracious are the raging but beloved monsters of the fire.

The Tartars of course respond, with their own rival fires, celebrations, and processions, on their own high feast a few weeks later. It is likely that, in most years, a perceptible number of citizens – adults, adolescents or children – will be mutilated, or charred, or lose their lives, or their homes, or their belongings, as a result of these bonfires (or malfires); but that is no more than a regrettable misadventure; the intentions of the pyromaniacs are comparatively benign – rejoicing and celebration, even if in part in mocking derision of the mistaken tenets of another sect.

But fire is put also to other and less friendly uses. Greek fire has long been known to the embattled communities and their factional armies. When a razzia is to be embarked upon, as likely as not fire will be brought in pots, bottles or boxes, and the homes of those attacked will be set alight. Whole streets, indeed whole quarters of the City, have from time to time been destroyed in this way: families fleeing, rescuing babies, pets, and what possessions they can, may leave behind skeletons of blackened and mangled brickwork smouldering still next morning. In other instances, it is the party forced to give ground to intruders which may set alight the street it is forced to abandon, rather than see it provide home and haven for the hated invader. In such cases, other mischiefs also may be encompassed before the petrol-sprinkled floor-boards are ignited: water-mains which might be used to dowse the flames may be cut or stopped off; newly mixed cement may be flushed down lavatory-bowls so as, irrevocably, to render the sewer unusable.

Fire is also used as a weapon of offence: against passing patrols of carabinieri; against the persons, as well as the homes and vehicles, of members of an antipathetic caste; as an instrument of economic warfare against shops, offices, factories, public buildings, places of entertainment; against omnibuses, trains, lorries, barges, ships, aircraft. Many and ingenious are the sophisticated tools of their trade fashioned by the arsonists of the City. And fire may be used, too, as a weapon of defence — for example, the blazing barricade that is designed to deter ill-disposed incomers, or the agents of unwelcome authority.

So besotted are the citizens of this tierra del fuego, that they have come almost to regard fire as an element heroic, and worthy in its own right of adulation and esteem. They derive from the πυρ or pyre, perhaps not wrongly, the concepts both of purification and of purgatory. They are not so far removed in spirit from the Zoroastrian fire-worshippers of ancient Persia, with their fire-altars and fire-temples: though not, of course, fire stations. For let it be noted that, in the City, the profession of fireman is viewed as a disgraceful one. When the brigade of sapeurs-pompiers attends a blaze, its members count themselves fortunate if they are not abused, stoned, or shot at, for their pains: even when they have taken the necessary precaution of coming by the longest way round, so as not to seem to be disguised emissaries of the hostile sect in the adjacent quarter.

OF SOUNDS, AND SIGHTS

The City is full of noises. It shares with other places, of course, the constant roaring and rumbling of traffic, and the whine of passing aircraft. But for those with well-tuned ears, there are other things to be heard. Not just the resonant calling of muezzins from the minarets, the sounds of chimes and peals and single bells; not just the constant mewing of gulls, the twitter of birdsong, the baying of countless (and often ownerless) dogs; but more sinister noises too.

The sullen crash of a bomb. The crackling of flames, the collapse of roof-timbers and the downfall of slates, the tinkle of shattered glass. The sound of shots, near or far, and then perhaps the sound of answering shots. Repeater fire: occasionally heavy-machine-gun fire: the firing of so-called baton rounds. The clatter of a hovering helicopter. The shock of a rocket hitting a moving jeepful of men. Home-made mortar bombs, striking in over the netting screen surrounding a poste de gendarmerie. The sharp crack of nail-bomb, blast-bomb, pipe-bomb, booby-trap. The deep roar of a land-mine. And, by way of accompaniment to all these sounds, the clanging bells and screaming sirens of ambulances, fire engines, security vehicles; perhaps also the blowing of whistles, the confused sound of voices high-pitched with passionate abuse, the clashing of dustbin-lids.

Not all these sounds are to be heard every day; or even, very often; yet, too often.

There are other sounds characteristic of the City. At certain seasons, the brash music of military bands, pipe bands, brass bands, flute bands, silver bands, accordeon bands; the rattle of side-drums and snare-drums, the thunder of enormous bass drums lacerated with whippy drumsticks, to the time dictated by a conductor playing upon a penny whistle. Other sounds again are the shrill and barely intelligible street-cries of newsboys; the variegated music, much of it melancholy and despairing, of itinerant buskers; the plaintive and (as it seems) never-ending ringing of burglar-alarms.

*   *   *   *   *

As to sights, the City is not especially renowned for the beauty of its buildings. It is, for the most part, a place of harsh red brick, dour slate roofs, and (for variety) dreary grey rendering. There is a sprinkling of buildings of stone, always imported. Such architectural showpieces as it possessed have, in large measure, been either destroyed by the greedy merchants, or nimbly mangled by fire, bullet, bomb. Gaunt hulks, shells, and steel frameworks, obtrude upon the eye. Over broad hectares of cleared ground, weeds compete with rubbish for a livelihood.

But all this is partially redeemed by the fondness of the citizens for paint. As previously remarked, each faction has its own identifying colours, and provided the observer has been trained to interpret the colour-coding, there are few places in the City where he need be long in doubt as to the sympathies of the locality. At the appropriate seasons of festival, gaily painted banners (their poles sometimes surmounted by wreaths of emblematic flowers) are escorted through the streets. Flags, gonfalons and pennants are hung from the house-fronts. Ornate and elaborate wooden archways are erected. These rites derive something perhaps from Renaissance masques, something from the fiestas of hotter climates. At all seasons, there are to be seen crudely painted kerb-stones, cabbalistic signs and exhortations on the carriageways, ritual emblems painted on gable walls.

Some of these paintings are tribal — their iconography, like their execution, is primitive and unsophisticated; but they are vigorous, colourful, and within the compass of a passably competent house-painter equipped with a sufficient number of tins of the primary colours. Others, however, are the work of more skilled hands – usually, art students; and represent, with embattled realism, scenes from local mythology, hagiography, or military history. The artwork is often supplemented by letterpress – exhortation, abuse, piety, vindictiveness; threats, aspirations, objurgations, manifestos. Many of these messages reappear as aerosol-brushed or crudely scrawled slogans on whatever vacant surfaces may offer themselves throughout the City.

Its square miles are none too rich in greenery, despite the best efforts of the municipal gardeners. There is always, of course, the ever-present green-grey-blue scrubby backdrop of the surrounding hills. Trees there are, though they pay a heavy tribute to each summer's bonfire season. Flowers there are, in the parks, in occasional window-boxes, in the florists' tubs; but few elsewhere – unless one may call in aid the ubiquitous dandelion, and the mysterious herbs which somehow flourish on bombed sites. The aspidistra population has dwindled sharply in recent years; but survivors may still be found; castor-oil plants, and rubber-plants, live a pampered life in the flashier office buildings. There is a bird-fruit tree in a populous thoroughfare, where at night small globular passerines try to imitate oranges and lemons. Although the climate is unfavourable, it is believed that occasional plants of oriental poppy and cannabis sprout indelicately in sheltered suburban back gardens.

One thing the City has in common with other places: the night sky. A low-slung winter moon may sometimes be seen hanging by a thread from the beak of a dockside crane. Stars, planets, satellites, meteors, comets, flying saucers, the Leonids and Perseids, all inch and etch their way across the darkness of the City, as they do all other places on earth, with utter neutrality, impartiality, and abstraction.

OF THE GOVERNMENT OF THE CITY

Many modes of governing this ungovernable City have been tried; none has so far proved wholly successful. With but a few exceptions, its leaders have displayed a degree of obstinate unreason not found in happier places. In this, however, they are but doing their duty, insofar as they faithfully represent those who chose them as their spokesmen.

Currently, the care of the City's affairs is entrusted to a Sebastocrator (or Governor) sent over from the adjoining archipelago; assisted by four or five Protosebastoi (or Constables) and an equivalent team of Logothetes (or Civilians); all these, colonial ministers and officials alike, being appointed not for life, but for specified tours of duty. By contrast, the Eparch (or Prefect of the City); the Stratopedarch (or Chief Justice); and the Protospatharius (or Commissioner of the Milices) are recruited locally; as are the Ulemas and the capped and robed members of the Court of Cassation. The Protostrator and the Great Drumgaire, commanders of military and naval forces respectively, are drawn from beyond the City. There are of course, in addition, numerous indigenous officers of state.

The arrangements for the representation of the opinions and prejudices of the citizens are of great intricacy and illogicality.

At one level, the City and its surrounding districts send over elected delegates, almost all Mongol and Sunnī, to the lower house of the Wapentake of the Eastern Archipelago; and occasionally persons of distinction are honoured by nomination to its upper house. Confusingly, one or two nominated representatives of the City from time to time sit on the benches of the upper house of the Majlis of the territory south of the stone mountains, despite the fact that it lacks any jurisdiction over the affairs of the City.

Moreover, by a subtle and fragile Transmontane Compact between the Eastern and Southern powers, the Sebastocrator has bound himself to consult with – though not to heed the advice of – emissaries from the Majlis, purporting to act as spokesmen for the outvoted Shī'a minority of the City. But this treaty has aroused the direst displeasure of the Mongols, who deem it treasonable on the part of the Governor.

At another level, an elected Council of the City Fathers, presided over by an annually elected Doge or Duke, though its powers are very restricted, does bring together delegates of both factions: although even in the happiest of times they tend to meet for purposes of mutual vituperation rather than cohabitation. However, the existence of the Transmontane Compact has caused the Sunnī majority, by way of protest, to suspend or adjourn over long periods all the sessions of the Council, without transacting even the most urgent business.

At an intermediate level, a provincial Diet having been

established with advisory and scrutatory functions only, first, the Tartar party indignantly refused to play any part in its heretical sessions; next, the Mongol deputies declined to perform the functions entrusted to the Diet, and used it solely as a vehicle for vociferous protestations against the Transmontane Compact; then, after patient persuasions had failed, the Sebastocrator prorogued it; whereupon, the most extreme of the Sunnī delegates constituted themselves a Secessionist Rump, and continued to hold meetings of protest against the Compact, not in the former stately quarters from which they had been respectfully evicted, frogwise, in the small hours of the morning, by the gendarmerie, but in the domed and minareted Municipal Divan of the now idle City Fathers.

None of these institutions has prospered, due on the one hand to the extreme disaffection of the Shī'a and Tartar minority; on the other hand, to the intransigent insistence of the Sunnī and Mongol majority that their wishes should at all times prevail, regardless of the susceptibilities of their fellow-citizens. There are indeed, at each of these levels of administration, a few moderate men-of-the-middle, ineffectual and high-minded; but these do not much commend themselves to the plebs, which on the whole prefers its consuls to resemble itself. Heavy, in consequence, is the burden which falls onto the shoulders of a dedicated petty bureaucracy bereft of leadership and of consensus.

Governors and high officers of state succeed each other in seemly progression. Their policies and personalities may differ, but whatever they do or say will inescapably attract the obloquy of one or other party in the state, often that of both; so that they tend to retire frustrated, exasperated, and as often as not discredited, after a short tenure of office. It is fortunate indeed for the people that, despite all discouragements, there still exist philanthropic statesmen in the neighbouring archipelago, and in the territory south of the mountains, prepared to throw energy, goodwill, imagination, delusions, imagined solutions, man-power, above all money, at the ineluctable dilemmas of the City.

In matters of minor and routine administration, a workable modus vivendi has, not without snarling and growling as between the opposed communities, been attained; but in matters of high policy, no such accommodation has ever yet been reached, or seems likely to be reached. All parties have entrenched themselves in positions from which no honourable line of retreat is visible. It would not be profitable to discuss further the arid politics of this particular Polis.

OF WORK, OR ITS LACK: AND OF RECREATION

The City is not free from an air of decay. It is not so prosperous and bustling a place as it used to be, even in the recent past. Though still a sea-port and a market, some of its trade has gone elsewhere. After many years of growth, its population is contracting.

Three generations ago, the City was noted for its manufactures: iron ships and their paddle wheels; machinery; malt; mineral waters; tobacco; intoxicating spirits; damascened gun-metal; and a range of coarse and fine fabrics spun and woven from jute, hemp, flax, wool, codilla and tow. Some of these trades have wholly disappeared; others are in chronic decline; only a few retain more than a spark of vitality. This process has weighed unevenly upon the citizens for, by long tradition, certain crafts and skills have been the sole prerogative of Sunnī's, others the exclusive property of Shī'as.

Nowadays, in the City as elsewhere, less and less work is devoted to the making of things; more and more, to the processes of marketing, the diffusion of information, and paperwork. The taking in of each others' washing, despite the growth of personal hygiene, has been degraded by the invention of washing-machine and launderette. As might be expected, however, there is a thriving black economy; frauds, fiddles, con-tricks, the double, the lump, all are rife to an extent which does much credit to the resourcefulness (if not the integrity) of the citizenry.

* * * * *

The principal recreations of the people are, in order of estimated popularity, watching television or videos; preaching or practising religion; copulation; and (despite the prohibitions of the Prophet) indulgence in alcohol. All of these pastimes may be enjoyed, in private, at home; but the City is also well provided with houses of amusement, houses of worship, houses of ill-fame, and public houses. There are moreover numerous hammams, swimming-baths, pool rooms, bazaars, amusement arcades, pavyons, oteli, lokanta, caravanserai: and of course the innumerable premises devoted to the various childish ball games to which the citizens are, endearingly, so deeply addicted.

There are also many quaint native sports involving animals, some not altogether free from cruelty: dog breeding, racing, and coursing; homing pigeons; trotting ponies; bookmaking; rat-catching; horse running and jumping; cockroach-racing; camel-fighting; bear baiting; coarse fishing; and so on. Each of these branches of sport requires its own fields, links, rinks, courses, courts, greens, tracks, or such-like.

There are numerous coffee and sherbet houses, kiosks, and places of entertainment where dancing, song, music and refreshment may be admixed in varying proportions. It is convenient and not expensive to get quite drunk to the sometimes melancholy strains of lute, rattle, gong, dulcimer, tambur, turkish crescent and tubalcain.

A minority of the population consists of persons of taste and learning, devoted to the study of incunabula; or Moghul miniatures; or puppet shows; or the janissarymusik; or the design of rugs or carpets; or ceramical lore. For them, the City provides palaces of display, medressehs, libraries, muniment-rooms, and gardens filled with abstract statuary and cylindrical tombstones.

SOME RESIDENTS OF THE CITY: 3

Tricky Micky and Bollocky Alecky are teenage burglars and muggers; nor are they above rape, if a convenient opportunity presents itself. They use stocking masks and dummy guns to impersonate members of one or another of the paramilitary armies, so striking terror into the old-age pensioners upon whom they mostly prey.

This is enormously risky; they are at peril not only from the gendarmerie, but also from the legitimate members of the organisations which they misrepresent; whose vengeance is not to be taken lightly. But from earliest boyhood, the two have been intrepid gamblers with life and limb. At the age of ten, they were adepts at the terrifying sport of leaping, ten storeys above the pavement, from the roof of one block of flats to the next. At the age of twelve, they had graduated to the more mature recreation of stealing motor-cars, and joy-riding in them at reckless speed around the adjacent streets, pavements, and front gardens.

They would not find it easy to obtain life insurance cover, were so bizarre a notion ever to enter their heads.

* * * * *

C'lette, D'nise, and the exotically-named Bare-knees* are three fine handsome and intelligent young women, now around thirty; though all from quite different sects and backgrounds, they have been close friends since together they took their degrees in psychology at university. They decided to put their qualifications, and their other talents, to good use, by establishing a non-denominational brothel. This they have done with great success: they cater with scientific skill for the varied kinks and whims of their customers. Sectarianism is strictly forbidden by the rules of the house, whether amongst the mesdames, their various part-time mesdemoiselles, or the clientele.

The establishment prospers, and the three girls grow rich, in a tall red-brick terrace house of many rooms, set in a discreet cul-de-sac (perhaps in this instance, con-de-sac) off a tree-lined avenue in a respectable suburb of the City.

* * * * *

Fitzy and Roma are the young partners in a mixed marriage. They fell deeply in love with each other, across the great divide, in their late teens. They love each other still; but the marriage is breaking down, and will soon be broken irretrievably if they cannot leave the City and take refuge elsewhere. Yet this is hard to do, for Roma's mother has a wasting illness and demands her presence daily. Unfortunately, the two families cannot abide each other: so deep is the gulf, that it proved necessary, not only to have two marriage ceremonies, but also two separate wedding receptions.

Fitzy's parents, ancestors, cousins, collaterals, are all entwined in a long and proud tradition of membership of the security forces, or the Sunnī and Mongol private armies, or even both.

*So pronounced; but sometimes spelled 'Berenice'.

Fitzy himself, as required by the precepts of his elders, has been enrolled in one of the more strait-laced and 'respectable' secret societies; also, without any sense of incongruity, in the ranks of the part-time gendarmerie. Moreover, he has a safe day-time job issuing firmans in a public bureau.

Roma's family belong to a very different tradition. Those few who are not members are nonetheless whole-hearted supporters of the Tartar paramilitant armies. To them, Fitzy is the very exemplar of what they have learned to love to hate. Even if they could somehow bring themselves to regard him as some kind of mentally crippled or diseased member of their tribe, they could never accept his relatives as anything less than hereditary enemies.

Fitzy and Roma first tried to make a home amongst his people. It did not work; she was regarded as spy, infiltrator, fingerer of honourable men; her modes of thought and of speech were not acceptable. The cold shoulder, and the colder innuendo, became unbearable: at her beseeching, they tried next to make a home amongst her people. It worked no better: he was regarded as spy, tout, informer, delator. They moved then to the twilight world of drug pushers, criminals and prostitutes, hoping to pass quietly unnoticed. On the contrary, they were more closely watched than ever, by the spies of both sides and by the gendarmerie too. Life for them both is as unhappy and frightening as ever it was before.

Roma is seven months' pregnant. What will become of her? What will become of Fitzy? What, above all, will become of their poor mongrel child?

* * * * *

Bob and Nettie, Tom and Hettie, Sean and Lettie, Dan and Betty, are decent, honest, hard-working couples, respected by all and with reason, bringing up their families on very moderate incomes but with entire success. None of them is much interested in politics; none of them is more than just conventionally pious; none of them belongs to any kind of sectarian or military organisation.

There is little to distinguish their habits or ways of life. As it happens, the first two couples are not acquainted with the second two; their paths have never crossed; but if they did, all parties would unquestionably behave with tolerance and perfect good manners. Yet the first two pairs are, by heredity and by up-bringing, Sunnīs, and are proud of their Mongol descent; the latter two pairs are Shī'as and of Tartar blood, and likewise proud of it.

Nothing on earth would induce even one of these eight honourable, intelligent and upright individuals to derogate from their ancient loyalties.

REFLECTIONS ON THE PRECEDING

Some of the citizens have confidence and optimism enough each autumn to plant the bulbs of hyacinths, tulips, daffodils, in pots or plots; and to prune back judiciously those bushes which are to burst into flower in a later season. Others prefer to live from day to day, almost hour to hour; if they may continue to see the sun rise each morning, that is enough.

For this is a community very deeply divided against itself; to employ the current jargon, 'polarisation' and 'alienation' between Mongols and Tartars, Sunnī's and Shī'as, are almost complete. In certain delimited arenas they can meet and mix – as in places of work, some sports and recreations but not others, some places of entertainment – but seldom without some stress, a degree of self-consciousness, a danger of a public clash. There is little mixing in private homes; at the end of a day spent in a mill, an office, a shop, the members of the tribes will make their separate ways to their several housing estates or dormitories, and there spend their hours of relaxation with relatives, school-friends, neighbours and colleagues of the same denomination and party.

The factions start from irreconcilable and passionately held convictions. Their perceptions of the same, neutral, event may be utterly different. Deep down, even the more liberal and broad-minded members of each believe that it is theirs alone which is in the right; that its members have been the victims of bitter wrongs, beyond all redress, over long years if not centuries; and that the members of the opposing sect may never, even dona ferentes, be fully trusted. And if such are the most intimate premises of most of the more reasonable, how much more extreme are the articles of faith of the most bigoted (who may yet also be the most idealistic) on each side. There is a degree of atavism about this; compounded by a helpless feeling of predestination, not confined to either tribe.

Yet, contrary to all reasonable expectations, the people of the City – of both factions – are, individually, as honest, friendly, generous, hospitable and sympathetic as any in the world. A person could easily spend a lifetime in the City and never meet a villain – provided he steered clear of politicians and clerics; not so very hard to do. There is a difference not just of degree but of kind between the citizens in retail, and in wholesale. Those same kindly family men who are so reasonable in private conversation change character on the instant when confronted with an election, a public meeting, a census, an opinion poll. It is notorious that public men and ecclesiastics, however conciliatory and moderate they may be over the private supper-table, will promptly repudiate their fair words if the press, or their own rank and file, be within earshot.

And this derives not from mere treachery or self-interest alone; but, in part, from the overpowering instinctive pressure not to display disloyalty to the clan. And in part also, from the knowledge that the constituents, the parishioners, the supporters, know very clearly what they expect from their representatives; and if any delegate should show signs of weakening, he will soon be jettisoned and replaced by another who is prepared to adopt a less compromising stance. And in part – perhaps the greatest part – it derives from the deep-seated fear of the other which runs through each of the two communities.

Otherwise, the City is, in private terms, as happy as any other place; arguably, far more so than a great metropolis where the links of family and clan have been submerged in isolation, impersonality and friendlessness.

CONSEQUENCES OF THE PRECEDING

So: what then? If this is a story, has it an ending? If this is a riddle, has it an answer? If this is an enigma, has it a solution? What is to be the fate of these extraordinary people?

*   *   *   *   *

The clerics and holy men will for the most part, barring accidents, die in their beds. Not so the soldiery, the fanatics, or their paramilitary followers. As for the common people, their endings will be inconspicuous, dramatic, humble, bizarre, violent, agonising or peaceful according to their respective stars.

Captain Buck Black will meet a sudden death by what is sometimes politely called lead poisoning.

Doc Pat will marry a beautiful, high-minded and strong-willed physician who will teach him to abjure for ever the treacherous proclivities of his past. But one night, armed men in urgent need of his skills to tend a wounded colleague will burst into his home, and endeavour first to blackmail him, then to compel him by force, to come to their aid. One of them fires a shot designed to intimidate him. By mischance, his wife walks through the consulting-room door as the shot is fired, into the path of the bullet: and all Doc Pat's Hippocratic skills cannot save her. His widowerhood is interminable, bitter, and filled with self-reproach.

The Ayatollah Omar will burst a blood-vessel whilst preaching. The moderate Hajji Ishaq will, quite unexpectedly, inherit a large fortune from an aged collateral relative. He will thereupon renounce religion, repudiate his faith, and thenceforward live in great comfort and cheerful godlessness in a pretty villa, set in a walled garden full of espaliered fruit trees, by a picturesque lake far from the City, served with sherbet and wine from Shiraz by giggling pert-titted teenage girls.

Silken Thomas will attain his doting century, amiably ambiguous to the last, loaded with laurels and honours, redolent of the bitter-sweet odours of sanctity and hypocrisy. The Shī'a Holy Suleiman will attain martyrdom, to his great satisfaction, for that is the fate he aspires to. But he will never know, and his ardent followers will never believe, that his death was in truth entirely accidental, and due to a faulty safety-catch: the presumed assassin having been kicked to death by the crowd without time to say a word in self-defence.

Of the three brothel-keeping bluestockings, C'lette will marry a rich bookmaker, becoming enormously refined and respectable. The repressed status of her vulgarian husband will be unenviable. D'nise will revolt against her mercenary way of life. A generation earlier, and she would have taken the veil as nun or priestess of an enclosed order; instead, she becomes one of the knobbly sybils of women's rights. Only Berenice will stick to the game:

she dyes her hair ever more vivid shades of red, resembling a maple in the fall; she drinks ever more lavish quantities of raki; she becomes (if she was not already) the jolliest and most popular Madam in the City. When she is found dead of a stroke one morning, her funeral turns into the best party that any of the citizens can remember.

Brother Pax Vobiscum will die, smug and self-satisfied to the last, in the infirmary of a chilly and none too clean home for aged clergymen. Brother Irenæus will be banished by his ecclesiastical superiors to a remote and scraggy mountainous parish far from the City, and there will eat his heart out, amidst a scowling peasantry, for want of a wider audience.

The marriage of Fitzy and Roma will go from bad to worse; there is nowhere in this City where they can both find happiness. A year after her baby boy is born, Roma is overwhelmed by blackest depression, and takes her life, using a combination of drugs, alcohol, and a transparent plastic bag held over her head by a rubber band. His finding of her body will completely derange Fitzy, who will spend the rest of his long life in an asylum. The baby will be taken into care; he will grow into a devious and malicious paranoiac. So that nobody will ever be sure whether, as he asserts at the age of twelve, he has been buggered by a pious house-father; or whether the house-father is the victim of a malevolent frame-up.

Brother Janus will be found dead in bed by, or with, his deaconess; accounts vary according to the tribal loyalties of the tale-bearer.

As might be foreseen, Tricky Micky and his friend Bollocky Alecky will not last long. The former will be shot dead while driving a powerful stolen car at high speed through a road block, his foot flat down on the accelerator. The lamentations of his clan are loud and indignant: but Micky, for a bet, was trying to see how many gendarmes, like skittles, he could knock over with one throw: so the sergeant who shoots him had not much choice or hesitation. Soon after this happening, Alecky, now operating alone as practitioner of robbery, assault and rape, will impersonate a paramilitant once too often. He will be hauled before a court of summary justice, composed of grim stocking-masked figures seated behind a deal table in the return room above a back street shop: condemned to death: and executed there and then, shot in the nape of the neck, his body casually dumped in an adjacent alleyway pour encourager les autres.

Nor is longevity to be the fate of Billy, William, or Liam, the three explosives artificers. William will be terribly maimed in the process of trying to defuse one of Liam's cleverest and most complex artifacts. But he will survive miserably, in a wheel-chair, for some years, having lost his eyesight, most of his hearing, the use of one hand, one leg at the ankle and one above the knee, and his testicles. Billy will be cut short untimely by a wholly fortuitous motor accident entirely unconnected with his profession. Liam will be killed – instantly, and so almost painlessly – by one of his own confections. Relaxing amongst friends and somewhat less than sober, he will be called upon at short notice to prime and arm a bomb designed to murder a potentate paying an unannounced visit. Usually the most cautious of men, this time Liam will be the victim of his own tipsiness.

Uel (affectionate diminutive for Samuel) will be shot dead on his own doorstep by a member of a rival army. Drew (affectionate diminutive for Andrew) will be sent down for a twenty-year term in prison for a crime he had not in fact committed: fair retribution though for the numerous crimes he did commit. Wesley will go into politics, become a populist member of the Diet for an enthusiastically partisan arrondissement, wheel, deal, and feather his nest very prettily, but lose none of the affection of his supporters on that account. Winston will, to his own surprise, be overwhelmed by remorse for the murders he has committed; will seek the consolations of religion; and will ultimately found a sect of his own.

The Archimandrite Chrysanthemos, in permanent retreat in an Eventide Home for Pious Silvertops, will munch, dote, and mumble, no more and no less useful to his fellow-men than when he was in his prime.

Pius will be ensnared by his excessive sexuality into an entanglement with a very pretty young woman sent expressly to seduce him. His pillow-talk having compromised his employers, they will set out to eliminate him as suspected tout or informer. To save his skin, he will become just that. Having borne witness against his former colleagues, he will be spirited away (for his own protection) to a distant country where, uncomfortable in the ill-fitting skin of a new and artificial identity, he will eke out a frugal and fragile life in constant terror of exposure and revenge. Innocenta, herself discredited by his treason, will slide by degrees into amateur prostitution; will bear, and neglect, several children by different fathers; and will develop her innate tendency to sluttishness to the utmost of its potential. Indeed, it will be almost a happy release when she is taken off by pneumonia.

Bob and Nettie, Tom and Hettie, Sean and Lettie, Dan and Betty, will never in fact meet each other; nor will any of them alter their loyalties one iota. Having each abstained from over-indulgence in drugs, politics, or religion, they will all live happily ever after: or as nearly so as real life allows of.

CONCLUSIONS OF THIS BOOK

So much for the residents: what does the future hold for the City itself? It is certain that there are no easy solutions, perhaps no solutions at all, to its problems. The foreseeable possibilities are not unlimited.

If, by one means or another, the fears which the citizens entertain of each other could but be dispelled, then it might become conceivable that the prejudices and postures of the past could be swept away. It is not easy to see how that is to come about, short of the appearance of an amazing new religion, or an astounding new transcendental philosophy.

Otherwise, it is not quite impossible that things may go in the City for another century, or two, or three, much as they have done in the past. That would not be a very happy outcome; but then, the alternatives are mostly unhappier still. And such a future depends, in large degree, on the continued benevolence of the peoples of the adjoining state and archipelago. But if they were unwilling to persevere, and if they withdrew their aid and presence, the results might be bloodier and more violent than anything that has happened in all the years that have gone before.

Perhaps the Mongol majority, in despair as to the integrity of its own future existence, might wage unlimited war to the death on every citizen of the Tartar minority; in which case, the fortunate few might be expelled or make good an escape; but – and there really can be little doubt of it – very many thousands of Tartars would be killed, burned, maimed, exterminated: and not much quarter might be shown to women, pensioners, children. Such a jihad, however dreadful, would not be without its precedents; it would be effectual and, perhaps, conclusive.

Alternatively, the Tartar minority might embark upon the forlorn expedient of a Rising, perhaps to correspond with an emotive religious feast-day: its volunteers might occupy with arms, by surprise, the Head Post Office; the Medical School; Transport House; Behan's Mill; the Biscuit Bakery: and other tactical strongholds. Perhaps, even, its leaders might read from the steps a proclamation 'in the name of Allah and of the dead generations'. The adventure would surely be overwhelmed, and those of the insurgents not killed in the fighting would surely be executed. From that over-reaction, there might – just might – flow such a revulsion on the part of the citizens, Mongol and Tartar both, as would overturn all that had gone before. But that would be a gamble against long odds indeed.

Last, but perhaps not least likely, the City may bring about its own utter downfall. Babylon, that great city, is fallen, is fallen. The walls of Jericho tumbled down at the blast of a trumpet. Troy lies hidden for ever under its nine-times mound. Deleta est Carthago. The sands of the desert, and the thin grasses of the steppe, have buried half the cities and half the civilisations of central Asia. Pompeii is buried under ash, pumice, and soot. Sodom and Gomorrah were utterly consumed, and even their refugees were turned into pillars of salt.

If all these are fallen, how: and why: and for how long: shall our City survive?